The GINGERBREAD MAN LOOSE on the FIRE TRUCK

Laura Murray · illustrated by Mike Lowery

SCHOLASTIC INC.

To my mom, Shirley, and my dad, Doug—
So much of who I am and what I strive to be
is a reflection of your love, encouragement, and guidance.
Thank you! With love, your youngest crumb-snatcher.

And a special thanks to the Fairfax County Fire and Rescue
Station # 1, McLean, Virginia—for your outstanding service
to our community, and your enthusiastic help
as I researched details of this book.

—L.M.

To my most favorit-est people
in the whole wide world:
Katrin and Allister.

—M.L.

ISBN 978-0-545-78247-0

12 11 10 9 8 7 6 5 4 3 2 1   14 15 16 17 18 19/0

Printed in the U.S.A.   40

First Scholastic printing, October 2014

Design by Ryan Thomann
Text set in Bokka and Dr. Eric, with a bit of hand-lettering
The illustrations were rendered with pencil, traditional screen printing, and digital color.

The **pocket** was cozy.
I peeked from the **top**.

The **bus** drove for miles,
then came to a **stop**.

In front of a building with shiny red **doors**
stood two **firefighters** from **Company Four**.

One had on **gear** for a quick **demonstration,**
and standing beside him was **Spot,** the **Dalmatian.**

I was **jostled** and **jiggled** as kids moved about.
Then I fell from the **pocket,**

Spot sniffed at my face, taking one sticky **lick**.

I needed a **TRICK** to get out of there **QUICK!**

He **tossed** me up high with his mouth open **wide**,

but I **flipped** toward his tail and slid down, like a **slide**.

My feet hit the **ground**. I took off for the **station**,

but right on my **heels** was that hungry **Dalmatian**.

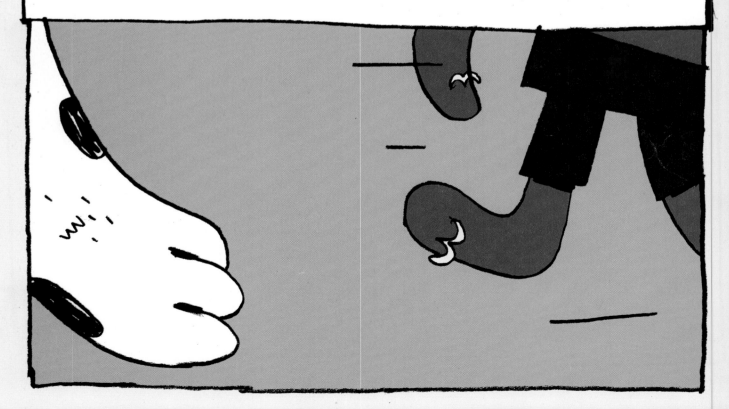

The class didn't notice. They tried on black **boots,**

and helmets, and air tanks, and big heavy suits.

I dashed to the **fire truck,**
jumped in a **Seat.**

I hopped on the steering wheel, gave it a **spin**— and yelled **out**

HONK HONK!

with a big cookie **grin**.

The wheel spun past **gauges** and **switches** and **knobs**— and all kinds of **buttons** that do different **jobs**.

Then I heard someone **whistle.**
Spot trotted away,

So I **jumped** through the window
without a **delay.**

I landed on top of a big silver **bowl.**

OH NO!

I cried **out**
as I leapt for a pole.

SPOT

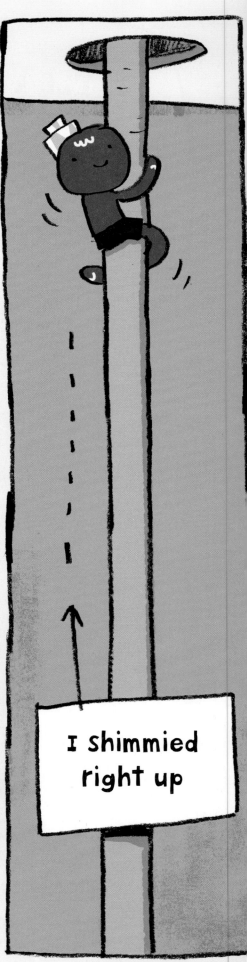

I shimmied
right up

and I **sprang** from the **top**,
then jumped on a bed

with a big
BELLY
FLOP.

There were several more bunks with their covers pulled **tight**
for each **firefighter** who stayed through the **night.**

I **bounced** on each bed on my way to the **door,**
then into a room with a bright checkered **floor.**

I peeked 'round the **corner** and smelled something **yummy—**

a grumbling sound rumbled up from my **tummy.**

SNIFF SNIFF

GRUMBLE

I spotted a fireman filling up bowls with **five-alarm chili** and buttery **rolls.**

Then all of a sudden, I heard a loud noise.

WOOOoo

FIRE!

one shouted.

NO LUNCH FOR US, BOYS . . .

They rushed to the BUNK ROOM and slid down the POLE.

I followed behind them, then peered down the hole.

WHEEE-EEEEE

went the **sirens.** The lights flashed **around**

as I **zoomed** past my classmates, below on the **ground.**

we sped through the streets and I clung to the **back**,

near **ladders** and **hoses** piled up in a **stack**.

The engine pulled up. Firefighters jumped out.
They rushed to the hydrant and opened the spout.

I spied a large house with a shed near the back.
Smoke rose from its window, all sooty and black.

I grabbed the hose nozzle and gave it a **pull**,

but that hose whipped and bucked like a rodeo **bull**.

The water **whooshed** out and it doused the old **shed**, and the powerful spray shot the hat off my **head**.

The chief ran up quickly and dove on the hose.

She crawled her way up till we came nose to nose.

LOOK, EVERYONE! IT'S A GINGERBREAD MAN. NOW, WHERE DID YOU COME FROM?

said Fire Chief Anne.

I CAME WITH THE CHILDREN TO VISIT THE STATION. BUT I ALMOST GOT EATEN BY SPOT, THE DALMATIAN!

We packed up the **truck** and drove back to the **station**.
We pulled in the drive to a standing **ovation**.

The children **applauded** and shouted out **"YAY!"**
They held me up **high**, yelling,

YOU SAVED THE DAY!

YOU'RE REALLY A HERO!
YOU'RE PART OF OUR CREW,
BUT YOU'RE MISSING YOUR HAT,
SO WE HAVE ONE FOR YOU.

"A SHINY RED **HELMET**
FROM COMPANY FOUR!

THERE ARE MORE FOR
YOUR **CLASSMATES**
STACKED UP BY THE DOOR."

I tried on my helmet and shouted,